INSIDE
OUTSIDE
UPSIDE DOWN

INSIDE OUTSIDE UPSIDE DOWN

by Stan and Jan Berenstain

A Bright & Early Book
RANDOM HOUSE/NEW YORK

Published in the United States by Random House, Inc., New York, and simultaneously in Canada by Random House of Canada Limited, Toronto. Library of Congress Catalog Card Number: 68-28465.
Printed in Melrose Park, Illinois, U.S.A. SP20001780SEP2020 Item #: 00001-636

Going in

Inside

Inside a box

Upside down

Inside a box
Upside down

Going out

Outside

THIS SIDE UP

Outside
Inside a box
Upside down

THIS SIDE UP

Going on

On a truck
Outside
Inside a box
Upside down

Going

6

Going to town
On a truck
Outside
Inside a box
Upside down

Falling off

Off the truck

Coming out

Right side up!

Mama! Mama!
I went to town.
Inside,
Outside,
Upside down!